FACE CHALLENGES,

ESCAPE

SOLVE PUZZLES,

BOOK

AND ESCAPE THE BOOK!

The Museum Heist

Published in French under the title *Escape book – Vol au musée*
© 2019 by 404 éditions, an imprint of Édi8, Paris, France.
Text © 2019 by Stéphane Anquetil, Illustration © 2019 by Maud Liénard.

Andrews McMeel Publishing
a division of Andrews McMeel Universal
1130 Walnut Street, Kansas City, Missouri 64106
www.andrewsmcmeel.com

21 22 23 24 25 SDB 10 9 8 7 6 5 4 3 2 1

ISBN: 978-1-5248-5593-2 hardback
978-1-5248-6752-2 paperback

Library of Congress Control Number: 2021930959

Made by:
King Yip (Dongguan) Printing & Packaging Factory Ltd.
Address and location of manufacturer:
Daning Administrative District, Humen Town
Dongguan Guangdong, China 523930
1st printing—5/10/21

ATTENTION: SCHOOLS AND BUSINESSES
Andrews McMeel books are available at quantity discounts with bulk purchase
for educational, business, or sales promotional use. For information, please
e-mail the Andrews McMeel Publishing Special Sales Department:
specialsales@amuniversal.com.

FACE CHALLENGES,

SOLVE PUZZLES,

AND ESCAPE THE BOOK!

The Museum Heist

STÉPHANE ANQUETIL

Andrews McMeel
PUBLISHING®

THE INVESTIGATION BEGINS . . .

Like every summer, you spend your vacation with your grandparents in a medieval town in Normandy, France. As if this weren't unusual enough, your grandfather also happens to be a security guard at the local history museum. You've always loved the museum, and one night you tag along on one of his night shifts. But as chance would have it, that night there's a theft! But what did they steal? And why did they steal it? Collect clues, question suspects, stay on the thief's tail, and discover the mysterious treasure they're seeking!

Solve the puzzles, chase the criminal, and recover the treasure by exploring the medieval town and its history!

HOW TO READ THIS BOOK

On the inside of the back cover, you'll find a museum map and a town map to help you find your way around. Both of them show you the main locations you can visit. You can move around freely using these maps. You don't have to follow a specific order.

Some numbers, however, have dotted lines around them. To get to these places, you'll have to solve puzzles using your smarts—and sometimes specific objects. You'll be told when you've "unlocked" access to them. And there are some locations that aren't on the map. You'll find them yourself over the course of your investigation.

On your adventure, you'll come across objects and clues **in bold** in the text. Like a **magnifying glass**, for example. You'll want to make a note of each object in your inventory, located in the back of the book on page **A3**, and keep track of each clue on **A4**.

When you are in a specific place and want to use an object, you can create a combination. You can find all the possibilities at the back of the book, on **A2**, and on the inside front cover.

How do the combinations work? You'll find some numbers in the tables. These numbers point you to sections in the book you can visit by using the corresponding objects. Some objects can be used in pairs, like a magnifying glass and a newspaper.

Magnifying Glass	Magnifying Glass & Newspaper	Newspaper
140	141	142

If you want to use the magnifying glass, you can see what will happen by going to **140**. If you use the magnifying glass and newspaper together, go to **141**. To use the newspaper on its own, go to **142**. Read these sections now to practice.

Beware! If you don't have an object in your inventory or it's not given as an option in your combination table, you can't use it.

Throughout the adventure, your cat, Professor Whiskers, will be by your side. He'll give you hints throughout the book. But this feline can be fickle, and his hints can be quite cryptic.

As you may have noticed, this book is illustrated. For some puzzles, there are clues hidden within the images, so pay close attention to those details.

Try to remember everything you can. . . . You never know what might be important! And don't hesitate to make a note of the clues—there's some space for this in the back of the book on page **A4**.

Have fun!

MUSEUM MAP

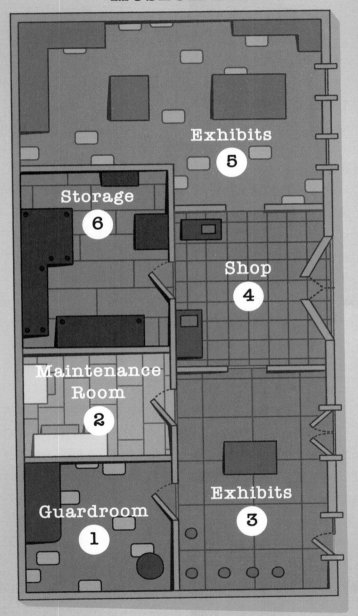

1
A NIGHT AT THE MUSEUM

You wake up to meowing.

"Shh, Professor Whiskers! Let me sleep."

"Meow!"

Oh, that cat! It probably wasn't the best idea to bring him with you tonight. Wait . . . that means you fell asleep on the job. And the guardroom is pitch black.

Your grandpa is usually the guard here. You've known this place since you were little, because you've spent all your summers in Normandy with your grandparents. They live in this tourist town, with the oldest part dating back to the Middle Ages. Outside the old castle, there are some shops and this museum.

While you've joined your grandpa on the job before, this is the first time you've been in the museum alone. As it turns out, this morning there's a fishing competition that your grandpa wanted to compete in, so in the wee hours of the morning he left work a little early and told you to take care of the end of the shift . . . solo. You were a bit nervous, but he said you were old enough and that it would be a good exercise in independence. Besides, nothing ever happens in a sleepy town like this.

Your cat's meowing again. He's getting restless and scratching at the door.

You listen. Footsteps! Someone's in the museum. What should you do? Ask who it is or shout for help? You didn't sign up for this!

The only thing you can see in the dark room is the battery-powered alarm clock, which reads 06:10. You reach out to grab

the big flashlight from the chair beside to you, but as you grope around in the dark, you accidentally knock it off the chair. It falls to the ground, making a loud noise. Oh no! So much for being stealthy!

You hear a muffled curse in the museum and the sound of someone running. Suddenly, wide awake, you jump up and hit the room's light switch—but nothing happens. Has someone cut the power?

You fumble to find your shoes and put them on in the dark. Then you find the flashlight that rolled across the floor. You turn it on and rush out of the guardroom. You're a brave one!

While you're not afraid of the old stuff on display in the dark, you need to see more clearly to collect clues and figure out what might have been stolen. So, before you do anything else, you'll have to get the electricity working again. To go to the maintenance room, go to **2**.

2

This is where the brooms, tools, light bulbs, and spare parts are stored for basic maintenance.

The fuse box is on the wall in a corner, with a small shelf beneath it. A fuse has been removed. No wonder there's no power! The intruder got rid of the right fuse by tossing it in with all the others. Ugh, how rude!

It's up to you to find the right one. Go check out the image on the next page. The fuses have numbers that will tell you where to go!

"They say that you shouldn't put your fingers in an electric socket, but this is an emergency! You can use your fingers to measure the space."

3

You can see so much better with the lights on! If you haven't already done so, go switch the power back on by going to **2**.

The room is full of shiny armor and impressive weapons: halberds, axes, and swords. There's also brightly colored knight and page outfits.

There's a mannequin outfitted like a medieval knight. Your grandfather affectionately calls him Leo because his coat of arms has a lion on it. He's dressed in armor and has a blue and yellow shield and . . . a sword? Oh no, that can't be right. You remember that the sword is being restored since it was starting get a little rusty.

On the wall, there are some historical engravings and a nice collection of French coats of arms. Each line of knights had its own for battles and tournaments.

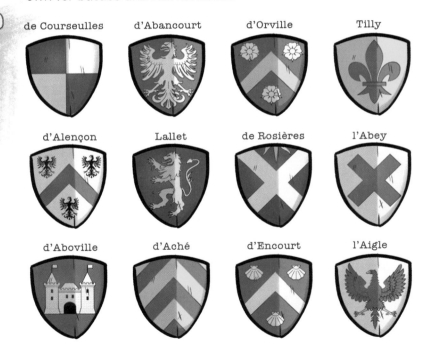

de Courseulles   d'Abancourt   d'Orville   Tilly

d'Alençon   Lallet   de Rosières   l'Abey

d'Aboville   d'Aché   d'Encourt   l'Aigle

In the middle of the room, in a display case, there are models showing how the town's castle has evolved over time. You'd love to play with them, but they're museum displays—not toys!

"Eagles, a lion, but no cat! I'm not impressed. The colors are pretty, though."

If you've visited all the rooms and know what was stolen, go to **19**. If not, keep exploring.

4

You're in the shop at the museum entrance. It's got a cash register. The double door is always closed and locked from the inside.

The shop sells tickets and souvenirs: D-Day memorabilia, military badges, model buildings, and even model knights!

The register doesn't look like it's been tampered with. The cash drawer is securely closed. They must not have been after money. You'll have to see whether any of the toys or other items for sale are missing. You can compare what you see with the video surveillance footage in the guardroom by going to **11**.

With the light on, you spot a balled-up **candy wrapper** on the floor. It wasn't there during your last round—you're sure of it. The place is cleaned meticulously every evening when the museum closes. This must be a clue! You pick it up, smooth it out, and examine it.

If you've visited all the rooms and know what was stolen, go to **19**. If not, keep exploring.

5

The helmets and weapons cast long, sharp shadows. It's frightening.

Did you manage to get the power back on before coming in here? If not, go back to where you were before!

You're in an exhibition on World War II, the one that lasted from 1939 to 1945. Clothing, photos, and unloaded weapons are on display. In the area around your grandparents' home in Normandy, everyone's got a war story. People like your grandpa experienced it, and they can remember the German occupation.

Before and during D-Day, bombs from American planes damaged the area extensively. After that, there was a lot of fighting, with Canadians, French, and Poles coming to help the

English and the Americans liberate France. For some people in the region, it doesn't feel like ancient history.

One of the mannequins has a **feather** by his foot, which seems out of place in the display. The plaque says he's an American aviator. You pick up the small white feather and examine it. It kind of smells like . . . chicken. Is this a clue? Did the intruder leave a feather behind while flying the coop? Stranger still, you feel the fresh morning breeze. The museum ventilation is carefully controlled to protect all the artifacts. You quickly follow the draft to its source. Someone opened one of the large windows out to the street!

But where did they go? You look closer.

A windowpane is smashed, and broken glass has fallen onto the floor of the museum. Once open, that large window would have allowed an average adult to get in. This must be how the thief broke in!

You take a look outside, using your flashlight to light up the street. You can see only the square. Some businesses seem to be open already, like the café and the bakery. The thief must already be long gone.

When you go to close the window, you notice a clear **footprint** in the flowerbed outside. Another clue!

When you take a closer look at the ground, you can also see some **ashes**. Are they from a cigarette? You're no Sherlock Holmes, so it's hard to say. But you should also remember this clue.

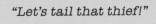

"Let's tail that thief!"

If you've visited all the rooms and know what was stolen, go to **19**. If not, keep exploring.

6

The door to the storage room is open. That's weird; you were sure it was closed when you went past it in your last round. The room is completely dark since there are no windows on this side of the museum. You wouldn't be able to see well enough with just your flashlight. But since you fixed the power, you can just turn on the light.

What a mess! Between the artifacts being refurbished for display and those stored between temporary exhibitions, there's cardboard boxes, piles of antiques in bubble wrap, and covered paintings. It's chaos. But it seems like something is missing. You can't tell what with all this stuff, so you'll have to compare it with the video surveillance in the guardroom.

PUBLIC
LIBRARY

MEMBER # 2334

If lost,
please call 31.25.62

But you do notice something on the ground near the worktable. A card. You pick it up to examine it closely.

And you know what it is . . . a **library card**! Yours looks just like it.

If you've visited all the rooms and know what was stolen, go to **19**. If not, keep exploring.

7

The space between the two prongs is too small. It won't fit.

You should use a ruler or your fingers to better judge the distance. Go back to **2**.

8

You plug the fuse in the two holes. . . . It's not easy. You have to push hard, but once you succeed, you hear the hum of the power coming back! Everything is well lit again.

Use the museum's map to explore the rooms and find clues. What does this break-in mean? Who's this intruder? What did they steal and why? But first, return to the guardroom by going to **11**.

9

There is a third prong that doesn't fit into anything. This isn't the right one.

Go back to **2** and try again.

10

The gap between the two prongs is way too big. It won't fit!

Go back to **2**.

11

THE GUARDROOM

This is where you dozed off after doing your rounds. You were excited about the chance to stay up late, and patrolling the museum at night reminded you of a movie you once saw (okay, so there weren't any dinosaur skeletons . . .), but pulling an all-nighter is easier said than done.

This room is in the far corner of the museum, hidden from visitors, with "Private" written on the door. Inside, there are four monitors and a video surveillance system. Obviously, everything is shut down since there was that power outage.

You find the **ten-euro bill** that your grandpa gave you on the table. You can always buy yourself something with it.

Once the video surveillance system has come back on, you try to rewind the video, but you have footage only until 6:00 a.m., apparently when the power went out. Everything went down, including the cameras. Yeah . . . it's not a very sophisticated surveillance system. What do you expect? It's a small-town museum!

You can sort of see the intruder breaking the windowpane and reaching in to open the window. Then their silhouette stands out in the dark. You can't see all that well. They've got a hat and boots or high shoes. They sneak in like a cat and enter

the room. Then: nothing. They cut the power. You don't have a lot of clues to start with.

But you can compare the rooms with what you see now to figure out whether anything is missing from the museum. Take a good look at the images on the screens before the theft and the state of the museum rooms now. Of course, the screens are black and white. This won't be easy—can you find what's been stolen? You can move freely around the museum by using the map.

"If I'd been able to spend the night wandering around the museum, I would have hunted mice in the storage room."

19

Adventure calls!

Suddenly, the phone rings. You head back to the guardroom. The ring of the old rotary phone echoes loudly in the empty museum.

You pick up the big handset with a feeling of dread. "Hello?"

"Hello, this is the police. Is this the museum guard?"

"Um, my grandfather isn't here. I'm covering for him."

"Is that a joke? We know the museum alarm went off. We will be there soon. And you'd better tell us the truth."

"Yes, I am. Someone broke through the window, came in, and cut the power. I just turned it back on."

"Be careful! Is the thief still there?"

"No. I scared them away when I woke up."

"Was anything stolen?"

"Yes, a sword."

"Well, be careful. I've been told that the gate to the medieval neighborhood has been tampered with. The iron gate has been lowered, and the mechanism that opens it has been damaged. We'll have to find another way to enter the tourist district. The thief must still be locked in there with you and those who live there. They'll surely try to blend in and hide the evidence. By the time we get there, it will be too late!"

"I'll investigate from in here, then."

"Be careful! We'll try to get there as quickly as possible."

So now, in addition to being responsible for guarding the museum for a night, you have to investigate the crime! You must rise to the occasion! Did you find all the clues in the museum rooms? Great! Now you can continue your investigation in the town.

You can now go to all the places on the town map except the ones with the dotted lines around the numbers. You've got to solve a puzzle to unlock access to those.

It's all up to you to solve this crime! The sun is already rising. You've got to hurry up and solve this crime before the police blame you and your grandpa! And remember—like in any police investigation, you shouldn't accuse anyone without evidence!

"Don't venture into the town until you've found at least three clues and you know what's missing from the museum!"

Welcome to our city!

Here, you'll find local shops
offering delicious specialties.

Visit our historical museum
and the magnificent castle
of the Dukes of Normandy.

Want to stay longer?

The Postal Hotel ★ ★
awaits you.

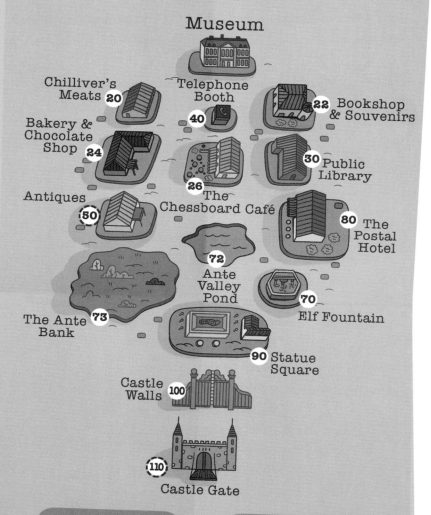

CITY MAP

Museum

Chilliver's Meats **20**

Telephone Booth **40**

Bookshop & Souvenirs **22**

Bakery & Chocolate Shop **24**

30 Public Library

Antiques **50**

26 The Chessboard Café

80 The Postal Hotel

72 Ante Valley Pond

70 Elf Fountain

The Ante Bank **73**

90 Statue Square

Castle Walls **100**

110 Castle Gate

The Postal Hotel: **31 74 50**
Chilliver's Meats: **31 21 33**

Antiques: **31 17 10**
Museum : **31 34 28**
Library: **31 25 62**

20

The metal shutter to the butcher's shop is slightly open. Bernard, the butcher, is already at work.

This is where your grandma shops. She's an excellent cook who makes delicious roast chicken. And your grandpa makes such good barbecued sausages. Yum!

You peek under the shutter, hoping he's not the thief.

"Hey there! What brings you in so early? I'm preparing some lovely chickens that were brought to me from the farm this morning."

You see little white feathers fluttering around him. There are even some stuck on his red apron. It's a little unnerving. . . . Then he lights a blowtorch! You are paralyzed by fear. What's happening? Is this a horror movie?

Bernard brings the blue flame to the chicken and burns the base of little feathers still stuck in the flesh. "I finish the plucking like this. It's better, especially for those who like to eat the skin."

Phew.

You chat a little with him. "Say, what time did you come in, Bernard?" you ask, innocently.

"I get here at 4:00 a.m. This is a job where you don't punch the clock. This morning, for example, I plucked the chickens. Then I took a little break to go have a coffee with friends."

"What time was that?"

"Well, at 5:30 like usual, with Gérard, the fisherman, and Michelle."

"Did you see anyone unusual?"

"No. Well—yes. There was an English gentleman who came to chat and drink coffee with us. Why do you ask?"

"Someone broke a window in the museum," you say. No need to elaborate.

"Vandalism? In our good town? Come on!"

"It's true!"

That's when Professor Whiskers, your cat, decides to join you by coming in under the metal shutter and meowing hungrily.

Bernard softens. "Oh, what a cute cat! Do you want some scraps for him?"

"Oh, thank you! That's very kind."

"Here, I always put some aside for them. And I have bones for dogs. I don't waste a thing. It breaks my heart to throw stuff out."

He comes out from behind the counter to bring a bowl out to Professor Whiskers. You take this opportunity to look at the prints of his white boots.

You also take a **bone** and add it to your inventory.

As for your cat, he's already devouring his meal from the bowl Bernard has kindly placed in front of him.

Meanwhile, Bernard talks about his passion for metal detecting. He finds metal parts in the fields, then he looks through the archives to identify planes shot down during World War II. He even goes as far as finding the pilots' American families. This hobby takes up all his free time. Something suddenly clicks for you.

"So, Bernard, when you find the airplane remains, do you keep anything?"

"No. Legally, none of it belongs to me. I hold on to a few pieces until I can identify the owner. The uniforms with their badges and stripes and the paintings of aircraft numbers help me a lot. After that, either I return the parts to the families or they go into our museum."

"Doesn't that bother you? You're the one who finds all these objects, and you end up with nothing."

"Well, sometimes I see a cap with its squadron badge in good condition and think I'd like to keep it. But I'd rather it be in the museum, where your grandfather's the guard, so that everyone can see and appreciate it."

"Thank you, Bernard."

To keep exploring the town, go back to the map and pick where you'd like to go next.

22

Like in most small towns, the bookshop sells stationery, souvenirs, and small toys.

There's a book on chess in the display window. It's opened to a page showing the names and positions of all the pieces at the beginning of the game. You can see that there are two sides, a black one and a white one. And there are two halves of the board, one half for the kings (the piece that has a cross on the crown) and one for the queens on the left. The placement of the pieces is repeated in each part of the board, with all the pieces— like the rook, the knight, and the bishop—belonging to a player side (black or white) and a side of the board (king or queen).

BLACK SIDE

Queen Side   King Side

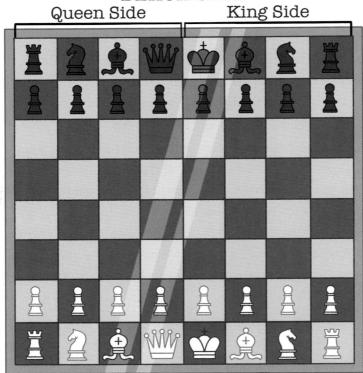

Rook   Knight   Bishop   Queen   King   Bishop   Knight   Rook

WHITE SIDE

But the shop is closed. You tell yourself you don't need anything else here anyway. As you're about to leave, you step on a big, brand-new **paper clip**. Someone must have bought stationery and dropped it on the way out. You pick it up absentmindedly and make a note of it in your inventory.

"There are four possible squares for horses but none for cats! Pity—black and white really suits me."

To keep exploring the town, go back to the map and pick where you'd like to go next.

24

The baker is already at work, and the bakery is open for early morning customers. You push open the door, and the bell rings.

The smell of pastries hits you as soon as you enter. In addition to the town regulars, the bakery gets a lot of business from tourists and visitors from the museum and castle. It has two specialties for sale: Arlette's shortbread cookies and William's delicious chocolate candy. You see the boxes on the shelves, wrapped in beautiful ribbon.

Sonia, the young baker who recently took over the shop, welcomes you with a smile.

"Good morning! Hot baguettes will be out of the oven in two minutes."

"Um . . . I'll have a chocolate croissant, please." (You can't resist, and it would be suspicious if you didn't buy anything.)

"I'm looking for someone who really likes your candy. Do you know who that might be?"

"Oh, that's Gérard, the fisherman! He eats it all the time—against his dentist's advice!"

"Have you seen him this morning?"

"Yes, he bought another box."

"And aside from him?"

"Not anyone in particular. But I didn't leave the bakery. I can't leave the oven unattended. So I have to stay here and have the lady from the café come and bring me coffee."

"Oh, okay. Mmm . . . your chocolate croissant is delicious!"

"Thank you. Here's your change."

As you lean over to collect your change, you notice her footprints in the flour.

Remember to make a note of **coins** in your inventory if you haven't already. You still might have a use for them!

To keep exploring the town, go back to the map and pick where you'd like to go next.

26

The small-town café has changed a lot in recent years. It used to be a place for old people to read the paper, but since it was taken over by a younger owner from the city, it's attracted a younger clientele. The only thing that hasn't changed is its name: the Chessboard Café. No one's around this early.

There's a local newspaper on the counter. To read parts of it, go to **A1** at the end of the book. To take it with you, you'll have to buy it.

When you look closely, you see that there's a table that hasn't been cleared. There are four cups that still have a little coffee in them. The ashtray's got a still-smoldering cigar butt. There are other clues too. . . . Take a good look at the next page!

The café owner comes over to clear the table.

"Good morning! Can you tell me who was sitting at this table?"

"The usual: Bernard, the butcher, and a couple of tourists on vacation in the town—Michelle, the painter, and Gérard, a fisherman. There was also a stranger who had coffee with them. A nice-looking guy with a mustache and a hat who invited himself to their table. Why do you ask?"

You improvise to avoid suspicion. "Someone broke a window at the museum. I was wondering whether there may have been a witness."

"Oh, that's odd," she replies absentmindedly before disappearing behind the counter.

"Who else is already up and about in town at this hour?"

"I just came back from bringing the baker a strong coffee. She's already working the ovens. Sorry, but I've got work to do."

"Okay. Thank you very much!"

Remember that you can always buy things with that money your grandpa gave you.

You can buy the newspaper by going to **27**, you can buy the matches by going to **29**, or you can have a nice hot chocolate by going to **28**. You even have enough money for all of that.

To keep exploring the town, go back to the map and pick where you'd like to go next.

27

You buy today's newspaper. You can read excerpts from it at the end of this book, on page **A1**. You can also use it as paper in your combinations. Make a note of it in your inventory as well. You can fold a sheet of **newspaper** into a paper airplane or roll it into a ball to play with your cat. . . .

You get some coins back as change, so make a note of the **coins** in your inventory, if you haven't already.

To keep exploring the town, go back to the map and pick where you'd like to go next. To buy something else, go back to **26**.

28

"A hot chocolate, please!"

"With cream?" she asks.

"Yes. Why not?"

"Just how the locals do it!"

Mmm, it's so good. And it wakes you right up! Now you're feeling ready to solve this crime. You still have some change. Check off **coins** in your inventory, if you haven't already.

To keep exploring the town, go back to the map and pick where you'd like to go next. To buy something else, go back to **26**.

29

"A box of matches, please, ma'am."

And there you have it! You could ignite some gas or burn your fingers, so be careful!

Be sure to check off **matches** and **coins** in your inventory, if you haven't already.

To keep exploring the town, go back to the map and pick where you'd like to go next. To buy something else, go back to **26**.

30

The library is where you typically spend your Wednesday afternoons reading. Comics, science fiction, detective novels, magazines—they've got everything! Elisabeth, the librarian, loves books and lets out a playful sigh every time you're late to return a long novel. But be careful—she doesn't hesitate to call out the rowdy kids. In any case, the library is still closed at this time in the morning.

There's a poster. "The library is open Monday to Saturday from 10:00 a.m. until 5:00 p.m., except on public holidays. To extend a due date, please have your library card number ready."

There is a code lock on the burgundy-red door. You'd seen Elisabeth punch in a code one day when you got there before the library was open. But you were polite and didn't look at the keypad.

She'd hesitated for a moment. You remember hearing four beeps. Do you remember what Elisabeth told you? "Fortunately, I got to choose the code myself. I have trouble remembering numbers. It gets embarrassing with my bank card. What do you expect? I am a woman of letters!"

You're not going to try numbers at random. There's a way to figure out the right code for this lock. Elisabeth must have used numbers that she knows by heart, numbers that are easy for her to remember, like a birthday or an event.

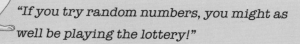

"If you try random numbers, you might as well be playing the lottery!"

Go to your combination table to try out codes. If you don't have a clue that can help you yet, keep exploring the town and come back later.

31

You hear a loud noise. Oh no! Luckily, nobody responds. Maybe you should avoid the #.

Go back to **30** and try again.

32

You punch in the code, but it doesn't work.

Go back to **30** and try again.

33

That worked! Obviously, the librarian's lucky numbers were the right code. I guess you've got to read the local paper, even though it seems old-fashioned.

The high ceilings and vaults feel even more impressive in this silence. The library used to be a hospital back in the Middle Ages.

You know this place well: the tidy shelves and the corner of colorful ottomans and stools for little kids. But you don't have time to read now. You've got to go to the librarian's desk and figure out whom the library card belongs to!

You move the mouse and discover that the computer was only on standby. That's not very environmentally friendly, but at least it's not locked. You just have to run a search on the card number. Get to work, young detective!

Go to your combination tables to enter the library card!

34

You don't have to try all the numbers; there's bound to be an additional clue somewhere.

After all, if the librarian chose the code, maybe it was a date or some other combination of numbers that's important to her.

Go back to **30** and try again.

35

You hear beeping everywhere. And then a blaring sound. Nobody responds, though. You think you might have one number too many! Remember what the librarian did when she opened the door.

Go back to **30** and try again.

36

The computer makes an unpleasant beep and displays the following message.

"Error. Invalid membership number."

You have to be more careful what you type!

Go back to **33** and try again.

37

The computer makes an unpleasant beep and displays the following message.

"Error. Membership number not assigned."

It can't be a random number. You must have found a clue somewhere.

Go back to **33** and try again.

38

The computer does a quick search then displays this result.

| First name | Address | Profession | Telephone | Currently borrowing |
| Christian | 50 | Antiques dealer | 31.17.10 | Norman Heraldry |

Very interesting. You have now unlocked access to the antiques shop. To go there, go to **50**. Or you can keep exploring, make a note of it, and go there later.

39

The computer searches its database then displays this result.

| First name | Address | Profession | Telephone | Currently borrowing |
| Stéphane | 74 | Writer | 90.15.22 | Jokes and Pranks |

You now have access to a new address. To go there, go to **74**.

40

Well, this is an antique! Can you imagine the time before cell phones, when all phones had to be connected by wires? You even needed an extension cord to go talk in the yard. And when people left their homes, that was it. No more phones. So if they needed to call from the street, in town, they used telephone booths. It's a great way to alert emergency services or to make an anonymous call, like in old crime movies where a character puts a coin in the slot and can make a call. Yes, one coin, like a vending machine.

In the phone booth, there's a faded directory with ads and most of the telephone numbers in the town.

The Postal Hotel: **31 74 50**
Chilliver's Meats: **31 21 33**

Antiques: **31 17 10**
Museum : **31 34 28**
Library: **31 25 62**

To make phone calls, you'll need coins. You can use your combination tables to choose whom you want to call.

You don't have any **coins**? That's frustrating. Maybe you should go buy something and get some change. If you don't have any coins, keep exploring the town. Go to the map and pick where you'd like to go next.

41

"Hello? Chilliver's Meats butcher shop. Um . . . how can I help you? Is this a wrong number again? Hello?"

You had no idea what you were supposed to say.

If you haven't already been to see Bernard, the butcher, you can go to his shop by going to **20**. Or you can keep exploring the town by going back to the map and picking where you'd like to go next. Or you can go back to **40** and try again.

42

The line is giving you a busy signal. It seems like the person on the other end either is already talking on the phone this early or didn't hang up their phone properly. Weird.

You can keep exploring the town by going back to the map and picking where you'd like to go next. Or you can go back to **40** and call someone else.

43

"This is the public library. We're open from 10:00 a.m. to 5:00 p.m. and closed on Sundays. To extend a due date, please call back during opening hours. We do not check messages. Beeeeeep."

That was the answering machine!

You can keep exploring the town by going back to the map and picking where you'd like to go next. Or you can go back to **40** and call someone else.

44

If you've already been to the hotel, go to
47. If you haven't, keep reading.

The phone rings three times before someone answers.

"This is the Postal Hotel. Hello."

"Yes, I . . . um. . . . Are you open?" you improvise.

"Obviously!"

"I'm looking for a tourist, maybe a foreigner, who may have lost something. Any idea who that could be?"

"Yes, of course! It's pretty quiet at the moment—the early birds have left, and everyone else is still sleeping. But you can come by."

"Thank you."

You can keep exploring the town by going back to the map and picking where you'd like to go next. Or you can go back to **40** and call someone else.

45

The phone rings and rings. It makes sense. If you're supposed to be watching the museum and you're in the phone booth, then nobody is at the museum. But nothing is stopping you from going back there to check that you haven't forgotten anything.

To go back to the museum, go to **11**. To make another call, go to **40**. To keep exploring the town, go to the map and pick where you'd like to go next.

46

"The number you called is not in service."

The coin drops, and you get your money back! Did you dial the right phone number?

To make another call, go to **40**. To keep exploring the town, go to the map and pick where you'd like to go next.

47

You change your voice to sound older.

"Hello, Postal Hotel? This is the gas company. We have detected a gas leak in your neighborhood, which could be dangerous. You should check the hotel's gas line to be safe. Can you go outside to look and let us know? Thank you very much!"

To see what happens next, go to **83**.

You can't just knock on all the doors of the town at random.

You may keep reading only if you've figured out how to unlock this area. If you haven't, go back to where you were before.

There's no chance you'd miss the place. It's got a big sign that says "Christian's Antiques." It's a beautiful old building made from yellow limestone. It's surrounded by high walls. The only opening is a large white gate. Next to the gate, there's a green chain that you have to pull to ring the bell. The shop hours are posted—it's closed right now.

Someone must be here, though, because there's a light on upstairs. You pull the chain, mentally preparing what you're going to say to the antiques dealer. You found his library card at the scene of a crime, after all. He's got something to do with this.

The second after you ring the bell, the sound is drowned out by aggressive barking.

A big dog jumps at the gate so aggressively that the gate shakes. You jump back in fear. He barks as much as he can. Gosh, this place is well guarded!

A dog is better protection from thieves than I am, you think bitterly. You ring the bell a second time, hoping that the shop owner will come, calm the dog down, and open the gate for you . . . but no one comes. And the light is still on. How strange. You still have to sort out this library card business. But before you can go in, you need to figure out a way of getting past the dog.

Take a look in your inventory and your combination tables and see whether you can find a way to get past this canine!

"Meow! The only thing we cats and dogs have in common is that we like to be fed. If you don't feed us, we'll have a bone to pick with you!"

51

You've got to wake up really early if you're trying to fish for a dog!

But only fish get lured in like that. There might be catfish, but there's no such thing as a dogfish.

Go back to **50** and try something else.

52

You throw some coins over the gate. You hear them fall on the other side. The dog stops barking long enough to put everything in his piggy bank. No, of course not. What are you thinking? The dog doesn't care about your money. He keeps on barking and barking. You'll have to think harder. You can collect your change on your way back out.

Go back to **50** and try again.

53

You throw the bone over the gate with all your might, as far as you can. Then you hear a stampede through the gravel on the other side. And no more barking. You risk opening the gate a crack and hear a quiet growl in the distance. You peek in. The dog is lying down and enjoying the bone you threw. He's busy.

Well done! You can go in now. Go to **60**.

54

You fold a sheet of newspaper into a paper airplane and throw it as high and far as you can. It goes up and up and then comes back down. The dog runs after the paper . . . and has fun tearing it to pieces with his sharp teeth. In two or three chomps, there's nothing but shreds left. Maybe that wasn't such a good idea.

The dog is annoyed and growls even louder on the other side of the gate. And you, you're still stuck on this side.

Go back to **50** and try something else.

60

You may keep reading only if you've figured out how to unlock access to this place. If you haven't, go back to where you were before.

To your right, in the opposite direction from the dog (which is convenient), you notice a large open door. This is the door to Christian's Antiques. The shop has been converted from an old secluded barn.

You hear a thud. Is someone there? You see a small desk with a cigar butt disrespectfully thrown into a teacup.

There's a thud again, followed by groans. It sounds like someone is locked in the cupboard! Oh no! He can't get out; he's been locked up—or worse, tied up and silenced. You try to open the door, but, obviously, it's locked!

Okay, you're going to need to find a big iron key. Oh, oh, oh! Well . . . there's certainly no lack of keys at an antique dealer's, which makes sense with all the old furniture.

Take a good look at the picture, and when you think you've found a key that matches the cabinet, go to the number on its key ring.

"Try to find the purr-fect match."

61

That's the label on a piece of furniture! Look for a key that looks like the cupboard.

Go back to **60** and try again.

62

That's the label of an item for sale! Look for a key, and pay close attention to the details in the picture.

Go back to **60** and try again.

63

That's the right kind of metal and the right style. Well done! You're an observant detective!

To open the cupboard, go to **69**.

64

That's not the right key. The color's all wrong!

Go back to **60** and try again.

65

This is not the right key shape. It doesn't match the cupboard style at all!

Go back to **60** and try again.

66

That's the right kind of metal, but that key style doesn't go with the old cupboard at all!

Go back to **60** and take a good look at the picture. Then try again.

67

That's the right color, but the shape of the ring isn't quite right for that cupboard.

Go back to **60** and try again.

Inside, you find the poor antiques dealer tied up. He looks at you with an expression of surprise and relief. You untie him while he stammers to tell you what happened.

"He tied me up and locked me up! In my own shop! In a cupboard! The scoundrel!"

"Who? I've also been on a thief's trail since early this morning. Someone broke into the museum! Do you think it might be the same person? Did you see them?"

"It was a strange tourist who tied me up. A guy with a mustache and a hat, speaking in a strong English accent. I saw him only twice. The first time was when he came by the day before yesterday. He was just like any other tourist . . . looking at paintings, hunting for knickknacks, checking out the furniture. I see dozens like him every day during the summer. He seemed friendly enough. We talked about a new lot of antiques that I got from Mr. Rigobart, an old man who was part of the resistance. This Englishman seemed passionate about history. So I told him about this notebook I'd found in the lot. I authenticated it as belonging to Mr. Ernest Dumont."

"Who is this Mr. Dumont?"

"Well, that's quite a story. He was a resistance fighter and the former owner of the town castle. During World War II, in the chaos before the Germans arrived, he hid paintings and valuable castle possessions left and right. Then, during the German occupation, Mr. Dumont was forced to let the Germans live in the castle. A requisition. The Nazis made it a command post.

Ernest pretended to collaborate. He took the opportunity to spy on German officers and to transmit as much information as possible to the Allies by radio. He was passionate about secret codes, and since he knew the castle inside and out, he managed to pass on information to the Allies. Unfortunately, one day he was caught, and he was never heard from again.

"In his will, he gave the castle to the city. In return, all he asked for was that an inscription be carved on the fountain. A story he made up. A little basic. It's the one you can still see in the town today. We found the paintings hidden in his home, but some of the castle's treasure was never recovered.

"And there, in his notebook, I found a draft of the story. Apparently, he worked on it quite a bit. He was counting the words, which is strange, because when you read the final version, it's pretty awkward and doesn't even make much sense.

"I showed the English gentleman the notebook, and we discussed it. He seemed interested. He asked me lots of questions, and then he left. Then late yesterday evening, he came back, claiming to have a breakthrough to discuss. Since I was curious, I let him in despite it being late. He asked to see the notebook again. So we came in here. And that's when he attacked me. He knocked me out, and I found myself spending the night tied up in a cupboard. It was terrible! And my dog isn't allowed in the shop—otherwise, he would have defended me and ripped the man's pants to shreds!"

"What about the notebook?"

"It's gone! Of course, the scoundrel took it!"

"Darn."

"And he also stole a book on heraldry that had my library card in it."

"What's heraldry?"

"It's all about knights' coats of arms."

"Oh, okay, there are some of those in the medieval room at the museum."

"Exactly. In the story, I wondered whether there was an allusion to colors: azure or . . . "

"We need the story."

"It is still engraved on the town fountain. I don't remember it exactly, but you can go take a look yourself."

"And what about the thief? Do you have his name? His address?"

"Mr. Douglas. But I'm sure that's made up."

"Good point."

"Okay, I need some food. I haven't had anything since last night. Then I'll go and file a complaint. Can you believe all this?!"

"Thank you. The police will be here soon, but they're stuck at the old town gate. I'll try to catch the thief and figure out what he's after."

"Be careful!"

Go to the map and pick where you'd like to go next.

70

Here, in the old part of the town, there's a fountain. The story goes like this: A young washerwoman was washing her clothes when the lord of the castle noticed her all the way from his tower. And he married her. Well, it's a romantic little story from the Middle Ages. Considering how high the tower is, that guy must have had great eyesight!

On the fountain, there's an engraved plaque with a strange legend about a knight and an elf who gives him his treasure. The writing is really strange. It's signed "Dumont."

The proud and strong knight was riding alone in the woods, the gold-colored sun warm and bright, the sky azure. An elf was hiding, there—practically right beneath him. It handed him a small chest, a box full of treasure, it seemed. But the knight had no key, and the chest was locked. He used his wits and his sword to pry open the box painted in black. Returning to his king with riches, he was grateful to have, on this unforeseen occasion, his sword by his side.

"Pfff, a story like that should go straight in the trash! Unless telling a story isn't really the purpose . . ."

Have you figured out what this means yet? Then keep exploring the town! If you haven't, you probably need to find more clues. Go back to the map and pick where you'd like to go next.

72

On the edge of the Ante Valley pond, which makes this part of the city even more beautiful, there are weeping willows with branches sweeping the edge of the water and ducks swimming in a row. At the edges of the pond, the grass is even greener. There are reeds where the ducks can shelter and make their nests. You spot a painter mixing paints not far from the shore.

"Hello there."

"Oh, hello! I'm Michelle. I'm on vacation here. I think I recognize you. Your grandfather is the museum guard, isn't he?"

"Yes, he is. Tell me, Michelle, did you see anyone in the town this morning?"

"Not many people, actually. I had coffee with Gérard, who lent me his rain boots. The edge of the pond is very wet, and I wanted to get as close to the water as possible."

"Oh, yes. I see your prints in the mud."

"They're a bit too big for me, but they're fine for painting."

"Who else was at the café?"

"Oh, a trader and a shopkeeper, I think. Though I pay closer attention to my surroundings than to people. The light coming through the trees, the way the sun shines through the clouds, the color of the sky—that's what I'm interested in. Besides, I don't want to mess up my painting. The sunrise should be spectacular this morning. Here, before you go, do you want some chocolate candy?"

She hands you a "William" candy wrapped in a pretty red paper.

"Thank you! Is this your candy?"

"No, I got it from Gérard. He's eating them nonstop. He really likes sweets!"

"Do you know where I can get more of these?"

"He'll be fishing a little farther away, on the Ante Embankment."

"Thank you for everything! Bye."

Go look at your town map and pick where you'd like to go next.

73

The narrow river is shallow and full of fish, and the water is crisp and clear. It feeds the Ante Valley pond, and it's a refreshing spot all summer long. You spot Gérard easily. He's wearing a ridiculous khaki-green fisherman's outfit. He left his footprints as he walked up alongside the river.

"Catch anything good?"

"Hey there, kiddo. Didn't you go to the fishing competition with your grandfather?"

"No, he went on his own. I had to cover for him. What about you?"

"Oh, I just fish to enjoy getting out early in the morning. I throw all my catch back. I'm not very competitive."

"You're not wearing boots?"

"No, today I'm staying on dry land in my shoes. I lent my boots to Michelle, a painter on vacation here in the same hotel as me. She's very nice."

"Say, do you smoke?"

"No, I don't. I like to take in fresh air. My guilty pleasure is candy. Especially the chocolate ones from the bakery."

"Oh, can I have one? I'm a little hungry."

"Sorry, I'm all out. I gave the last of them to my friends at the café. You could always fish for something to eat! Here, if you want, I'll lend you a **fishing rod**."

(Make a note of that fishing rod in your inventory!)

"Um . . . that's nice! But do you think I'd catch a fish right away?"

"I'm just kidding! Let's see. . . . If you're hungry, you could go to the bakery where I buy my candy. It's already open."

"Ah, yes, of course! The bakery. Thank you! Have a good day."

You're glad to have dodged eating raw fish. Go look at the map and pick where you'd like to go next.

74

You ring the doorbell at a pretty house. A man answers the door, grumbling. He's barely awake. He's in his slippers and pajamas.

"Hello, sir, I found your number in the . . ."

"Okay, enough already! Another lost reader? I can't help you all. Everything you need is in the book. Reread everything and check your notes. I was up late writing and haven't had my coffee yet! You're on your own! Goodbye!"

It might be better if you go back to where you were before.

80

You walk up to the small two-star hotel with white shutters and half-timbered walls—exposed wooden beams supporting mud walls. It's very pretty. Everything seems calm. . . . A service door opens on the side of the building, and a waiter comes out to throw a bag in a large dumpster. You watch him closely. When he opens the dumpster, you clearly see a pair of boots!

You wait quietly until the man is gone. Then you approach the dumpster and open it. Yuck! It smells terrible! Digging around in the trash is disgusting, but it's all part of being a detective. You take a close look at the **boots**. They're far too new to be thrown away! Why did the person get rid of them? They're a European size 43. You look carefully at the tread.

Next to the boots in the trash, you see a green hat and a fake mustache. Interesting.

You tell yourself that you should go into the hotel to verify your suspicions. Once you make that decision, you brace yourself and enter the hotel.

From behind the reception desk, the receptionist spots you. He looks at you inquisitively while he answers the phone. As soon as he hangs up, he addresses you. "Welcome to the Postal Hotel. How can I help you?"

"Hello there. I work at the museum, and yesterday someone left a valuable personal item while visiting. Are there . . . um . . . any tourists among your guests?"

"Gérard Pech, room 4, and Miss Michelle Eglantine, room 2. The Gauthiers were in room 5. That's a family with four unruly children. But they left early this morning. They had a long trip ahead of them."

"Is that it?"

"No, there's Mr. Gadulos in room 6. He's not a tourist, though. He's here for a business trip—working on the fireworks at the castle. And this morning he left without even having breakfast! So early that I didn't have the chance to wish him good morning."

"Do any of your guests smoke?"

"Oh, I'm sure. But smoking is prohibited in the hotel. The entire establishment is nonsmoking as a fire safety precaution. We even invested in a smoke alarm system that would trigger an evacuation if a customer were smoking. We are very strict about this. I plan to install an even more advanced gas detector soon—for all kinds of hazards."

"Oh, that's impressive. You're clearly very concerned about safety."

"Of course! If the hotel went up in smoke, I'd lose everything. And it's a family business. I do almost everything on my own, and I care about it more than anything!"

"One last question. Did anyone other than Mr. Gadulos leave early this morning?"

"All of them did, in fact. I served everyone breakfast."

"Well, thank you for your help. I'll come back later."

You did well. It's hard to ask adults probing questions. It wasn't easy, but maybe you got some useful information.

Since all the customers are out, you could search the rooms and find more clues. But there is still the hotel owner, who is right in front of the board with all the room keys . . . unless you manage to get him out.

How can you trick him? What about a false alarm, for example? It's not a very nice thing to do, but it would be a good way to allow you to check out the rooms in peace. How could you do this? A phone call maybe? Do you know a place you could go that could help you carry out this plan?

"The answer is as easy as picking up the phone!"

82

You may keep reading only if you've figured
out how to unlock this area. If you haven't,
go back to where you were before.

The person staying in this room has very nice leather suitcases with a name on them, Miss Eglantine. You also find a box of watercolors, a sketchbook with pretty drawings of landscapes, and a tourist guide to the city. There's a blue pack of cigarettes on the nightstand. The guest left a pair of high heels in the corner of the room. They're a size 38. What do you make of it all?

Keep searching the rooms for clues by going to **84, 85,** or **86.** If you're done searching the rooms, you can put the keys back and walk away without being noticed. Then you can keep exploring the town by going back to the map and picking where you'd like to go next.

83

You may keep reading only if you've figured
out how to unlock this area. If you haven't,
go back to where you were before.

You quickly return to the hotel, slightly ashamed of what you've done. But you remind yourself that you had a good reason.

The emergency exit door opens, letting out a panic-stricken cleaner and the hotel owner. They start sniffing around and looking for the nonexistent gas leak. You quickly go through the entrance, borrow the room keys, and climb the stairs.

You've unlocked access to the rooms! Which one are you going to search first? To search room 2, go to **82**. To search room 4, go to **84**. To search room 5, go to **85**. To search room 6, go to **86**.

84

You may keep reading only if you've figured out how to unlock this area. If you haven't, go back to where you were before.

There's a pair of well-polished shoes in front of the door to the room. They're size 41. The person staying here must be a quiet gentleman. His things are meticulously folded. Nothing stands out, except for the empty box of chocolate candy in the trash with that red "William" packaging.

Keep searching the rooms for clues by going to **82**, **85**, or **86**. If you're done searching the rooms, you can put the keys back and walk away without being noticed. Then you can keep exploring the town by going back to the map and picking where you'd like to go next.

85

You may keep reading only if you've figured out how to unlock this area. If you haven't, go back to where you were before.

You're in a large family suite with four beds. Everything is a mess. There are no clear clues. The cleaning lady has her work cut out for her!

Keep searching the rooms for clues by going to **82**, **84**, or **86**. If you're done searching the rooms, you can put the keys back and walk away without being noticed. Then you can keep exploring the town by going back to the map and picking where you'd like to go next.

86

You may keep reading only if you've figured
out how to unlock this area. If you haven't,
go back to where you were before.

Mr. Gadulos is traveling light. He didn't leave any shoes out. The things he does have are neatly folded. It looks like he likes to work and read in the hotel. On the small desk, there's a tourist brochure on the castle and a book on heraldry. It's the borrowed library book! It's open to a page on colors.

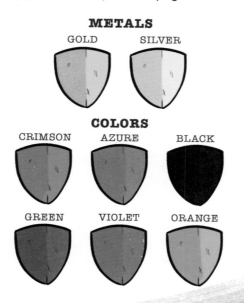

METALS

GOLD   SILVER

COLORS

CRIMSON   AZURE   BLACK

GREEN   VIOLET   ORANGE

That's not all! You find two more clues while going through the trash. It just goes to show that while rummaging through trash cans isn't sanitary, it's a good skill for a private detective to have! The first clue is a crumpled-up piece of paper. It's a strange list that makes you think of secret codes. It must be important!

Read backwards
First letter
Every other word
Every third word
Every fourth word

You also find a photograph of the castle. It's not a very pretty one. You understand why it was thrown in the trash. How mysterious!

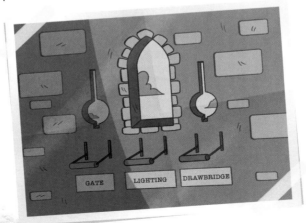

Keep searching the rooms for clues by going to **82**, **84**, or **85**. If you're done searching the rooms, you can put the keys back and walk away without being noticed. Then you can keep exploring the town by going back to the map and picking where you'd like to go next.

90

You're in a lovely little cobblestone square near the castle entrance. There's parking for tourists and a giant statue of William, the Duke of Normandy and King of England, on his horse. The statue's on a big stone base surrounded by six small statues of his six faithful knights. The statue is from the nineteenth century, so the historical details are a bit romanticized—they'd forgotten what that time was really like. But the statue is really something else! The horse is rearing up on its hind legs, so that must have been challenging to balance a bronze statue that big! Can you imagine?

The name of each knight is inscribed on the base. If your investigation has led you to think you should look at the statue of a specific knight, go try that by using your combination table. If you don't know which knight you're supposed to be looking at, keep exploring the town using your map, then come back later.

91

What a magnificent knight. He's got a helmet that protects his nose. You love the chevron coat of arms engraved on his shield. You can't see the colors, but you have a way of finding out! You can check at the museum by going to **3**. In this case, know that in heraldic language "red" is "crimson."

When you're done at the museum, go back to **90** and try again.

92

This knight has both hands resting on the pommel of a sword stuck in the ground. None of his parts move. His shield is a checkerboard, and it makes you think of chess. Unfortunately, you can't see its colors on this bronze statue.

You can check the colors at the museum by going to **3**. When you're done at the museum, go back to **90** and try again.

93

You carefully examine the statue of the knight. He's got a lion on his shield, which reminds you of the museum's coat of arms exhibit. You remember the coded message on the fountain also said something about azure and gold and a knight's sword being the key. So you examine the pommel of the knight's sword. It's decorated with a ring. That's weird for a pommel. They're usually round or diamond shaped. You try to lift it. Oh, it's moving! Part of the statue is coming out! When it's out, you see that it's a big key. Make a note of the **old key** in your inventory. What a discovery!

The elf's rhyme was true. What does it say next? A hiding place? There is nothing here under the statue, which is way too heavy anyway. Where should you go next? Where can you find a knight?

Go to the map and pick where you'd like to go next.

94

This knight has an ax in his hand and his coat of arms on the hilt of his sword. Nothing moves on this statue. Its coat of arms is the one with flowers. You might have the wrong knight.

Think about your clues, go back to **90**, and try again.

95

This knight's got style. He's got a hand on his hip and is posing with his shield on the ground. It has a bit of golden yellow sun just like in the story on the fountain. But no matter what you do or how closely you look at the statue, you can't find anything on it that moves.

Maybe it's that white cross that covers this coat of arms that you can see in the museum by going to **3**. This must not be the right knight. You were so close! Go read the story on the fountain carefully again by going to **70**. Maybe only some words matter? When you're done, go back to **90** and try again.

96

This one is holding a banner that looks like it's fluttering in the wind, just like his cape. There's a fleur-de-lis on his coat of arms. You know from the coats of arms in the museum that it's red and gold. That's not "azure." Think harder, go back to **90**, and try again.

"At night, all cats look gray! But during the day, you can see the colors. It's just like that with the coats of arms that you've seen before."

100

The castle has three levels of defense. It's got a moat, which has now been drained for health reasons—and stagnant green water and mosquitoes are not great tourist attractions! You go over the moat on the drawbridge. It's always lowered, except on special occasions. It still works, and the tourists love it!

Then there is a wall that goes around the castle. On the other side of the drawbridge, there's a large gatehouse with a large wooden gate. On the other side of that gate is the path to the castle. There's only one problem: the gate's closed.

The castle keeper isn't here yet. The tours don't even start for hours. But you've visited the castle before. You even know about some parts that aren't open to the public, because your grandpa is friends with the castle keeper. You know that the lever that opens the gate is just on the other side of the wall. And you don't want to be stuck out here.

To get inside, you've got to find a way to grab the lever and pull it up. Lucky for you, they've just upgraded the system, and it shouldn't be harder than flipping a switch.

Do you have something that could help you reach the levers? Take a look at your inventory and your combination table to see whether you can find a way to open this gate.

101

Do you think a sheet of newspaper might help you? You think that making it into a paper airplane and throwing it through the lancet holes would open the door? Maybe, if you were trying to communicate with someone. But in this instance, you're trying to raise a lever. Think harder. Maybe go fishing for some ideas.

Go back to **100** and try again.

102

The outdoor lighting goes out. That's not the right one! It's not the blue controller. Pay closer attention.

Go back to **103** and try again.

103

What a great idea! You can use the fishing rod to cast the hook through one of the openings and help you raise the lever!

Which opening should you go through? One of them will put the fishing line right above the correct lever to open the door.

Go to the numbered section in the picture to see what happens next.

104

You hook the green lever. The drawbridge begins to shake and rise, with you on it! You stop immediately!

Fortunately, you manage to unhook and release the lever by giving your line slack then reeling it in. How could you have gotten this wrong?

Did you take a good look? If you know the order of the controllers from the inside, how are they different when you're outside?

Go back to **103** and try again.

105

Using an old key to open a castle gate is a good idea. But this is not a gate that opens with a key. That key opens something else somewhere else.

Go back to **100** and try again.

106

That's it! The order's reversed. The red lever on the left of the photo is right under the lancet hole on the right.

The castle gate creaks open. It's not exactly stealthy, but it works.

You've unlocked the castle gate. Go to **110**.

110

**You may keep reading only if you've figured
out how to unlock this area. If you haven't,
go back to where you were before.**

You're not there yet! There's a solid wood door you still need to get through. This is hard! There's no way around this and no way of using brute force.

You know the right key is around here somewhere. Unfortunately, there's a whole board full of keys—at least nine! You have to be fast to beat the thief. And trying each one is not the fastest way.

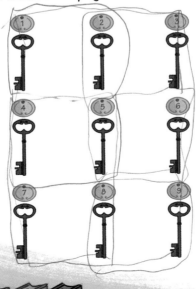

Your grandpa once told you a story. He had asked his friend the castle keeper which key opens the door.

The mischievous keeper replied, "The key's number is the same as the number of imaginary squares that can be made between the loops of all the keys on the board."

The keeper, content with his riddle, had refused to say more. Your grandpa had decided that he was messing with him, and, at the time, no one had tried to figure it out. But now this is important! Look closely at the board of keys.

See—you can make connections between the numbers. For example, if you draw a line from 1, to 2, to 5, to 4, and back to 1, you get a square.

So how many squares could you make altogether? Surely more than one.

Come up with an answer, add 110 to the number you conclude, and then go to that section to see whether you've got the key that opens the door.

"As a cat, I love to crawl into square boxes to take naps. That box needs to be just right— not too big and not too small."

111

You didn't quite get it. You can make more than one square when you connect the keys on the board.

Go back to **110** and try again.

112

Only two squares? Are you sure? If you draw a line from 2, to 3, to 6, to 5, and back to 2, you've got a second square. There have got to be more. Count again, carefully.

Go back to **110** and try again.

113

Three squares between nine points? Key 3 doesn't open the door. Try using a pencil to draw all the squares between the numbers.

Go back to **110** and try again.

114

Four squares? That's almost logical. You take key 4 from the hook and try it in the lock. It doesn't work.

To solve this puzzle, you've got to step back and give yourself some perspective.

Go back to **110** and try again.

115

You grab key 5 and try it in the lock. The door opens! Well played! You remembered to count the big square made from connecting 1, 3, 9, and 7.

Go to **120**.

116

You grab key 6. It fits easily in the lock. So easily that it's too small to open the door.

Go back to **110** and try again.

117

You grab key 7. No matter how hard you try, you can't fit it in the lock. It's got to a be a square, not just any rectangle.

Go back to **110** and try again.

118

You confidently pick up key 8. You manage to get it in the lock, but you can't turn it. It looks like you picked the wrong key. Take a good look at the picture!

Go back to **110** and try again.

119

Nine squares? Key 9 doesn't open the door. Remember that a square has to be the same length on each side.

Go back to **110** and try again.

120

The castle is huge. Everything is still empty at this time since the tourists aren't here yet. Your footsteps echo in the cavernous space. Luckily, the sun is now up. This would have been even more intimidating in the dark.

You feel like you're on the right track. Do you already know where to go? A small map shows you how to get to the lord's chambers, to the chess room, and to the dungeon.

"The treasure that Dumont encoded in the fountain story is close by. You want to check the right room."

To go to the lord's chambers, go to **121**. To go to the chess room, go to **122**. To go to the dungeon, go to **123**.

121

This is where the lord of the castle and his family lived. The furniture in here is basic: a few chairs, some simple planks of wood on trestles as tables, and chests that used to contain valuable things like linen, clothing, and dishes. It's all staged, though, something for the tourists. There's nothing valuable, no treasure, and no knights in here.

Go back to **120** and try again.

122

To go to the chess room, you've got to push open another heavy wooden door. It slams loudly shut behind you. These old things! How can you surprise a thief when you're making so much noise?

You go down a spiral staircase. And as quiet as you try to be, the sound of your footsteps bounces off the stone walls. Then you hear swearing and the sound of someone running. There's nothing you can do about it now, so you start running too! But you're too late. You hear a door slam in the distance.

You finally get to the chess room. To go in, go to **130**.

123

This is the last of the castle dungeons that's still intact. It was built in the beginning of the thirteenth century, when Philippe Auguste, the King of France, conquered Normandy. It's a military construction, designed for defense. It has its own well for drinking water. The passages are narrow. And it's got an amazing panoramic view of the city. When you look out, you see that the police have finally managed to get into the old town.

You've got to hurry up and finish your investigation! Go back to **120** and try going somewhere else.

130

Before you enter this room, make sure you have finished your investigation in town. Did you manage to get into the library, the antique dealer's, and the hotel? Have you figured out what the story on the fountain is about? If you haven't done all these things, go back! If you have, keep going. It's up to you to conclude this adventure brilliantly!

	136		138	132		135	
	139					134	
	131			137		133	

The chess room is aptly named. There's a high-vaulted, yellow-limestone ceiling and a large black-and-white checkerboard on the floor. You see an old sword nearby. You recognize it as the one missing from the museum!

You see that the thief must have lifted one of the squares to look for the treasure from the story. Since they were here only moments ago, they must not have succeeded. They heard you and fled. Now it's up to you!

Which square of the chessboard will you try to lift?

"I once took a nap on a chessboard. Grandpa complained because I knocked over all the chess pieces. But he knew how to put them all back in the right place."

131

This is the position of the white queen's knight. The white side is at the bottom, and the queen is on the left side of the board.

Go back to **130** and try again.

132

This is the square for the black king. You're on the right side, but not in the right square.

Go back to **130** and try again.

133

This is the square where the white king's knight goes at the beginning of a game. You've got the wrong color.

Go back to **130**, look at the chessboard, and try again.

134

There is nothing special about this square. It's the square for the pawn of the black king's knight. Where did you hear about a pawn? You didn't!

Go back to **130** and try again.

135

If you were playing a game of chess, this square is where you'd put the black king's knight.

When you read one word out of four on the fountain story, you get the hidden message: "The knight in gold and azure hiding beneath him a treasure. The key was his sword. The black king was on his side." You use your fingernails to get under the square and lift it up.

To see what's underneath, go to **150**!

136

This is the square for the black queen's knight. It's nothing special. The queen and the king each have a side of the board.

Go back to **130** and try another square.

137

You lift the white king's square. There's nothing interesting under it.

Go back to **130** and try again.

138

This is the black queen's square. You've got the right color, but the story is about a king and a knight.

Go back to **130** and try again.

139

This is square for the pawn of the black queen's knight. There's nothing interesting hidden there.

Go back to **130** and try again.

140

You peer through the magnifying glass, and you see tiny smudges of chocolate on the page. Go wash your hands before you keep reading. You get the idea.

Go back to the beginning of the book.

141

Using the magnifying glass and the newspaper together, you read some very small printed text: "Well done! You understand how combinations work. Now you can go back to the beginning."

142

You fold a sheet of newspaper into a paper airplane. It flies up into the sky, spinning.

You can go back to the beginning of the book.

150

Underneath the square, there is some kind of metal compartment with a lock. A secret safe! What do you think will help you open it? Take a look at your inventory and your combination table to see whether you can find a way to open the safe.

"The thief must have the hidden message. It looks like he thought he needed the knight's sword from the museum as a key. He was wrong. How about you? Do you have what you need? Where else are there knights, forever still?"

151

You've already used that fishing rod. And you can't use the hook to pick a very old and very strong lock.

Go back to **150** and try again.

152

This is not a locker at the swimming pool. That won't work!

Go back to **150** and try again.

153

You insert the old key you found in the statue of Knight Lallet's sword pommel. You turn it, and the safe opens. This is amazing! The safe hasn't been unlocked since World War II! Mr. Dumont's hiding place is finally revealed over half a century later!

Find out what happens next by going to **160**!

154

Are you going to try to pick a lock like in the movies? That won't work. The lock is far too hard! It won't open with a paper clip. Not a bad idea, though. Keep trying!

Go back to **150**.

160

When you open the safe, you find a beautiful old leather-bound book, illuminated with gold. You open it carefully. Delicate paintings in blue and red illustrate the manuscript. It's in handwritten Latin. It's a very valuable medieval book!

That's when you hear someone behind you and jump out of your skin.

"The nerve! A little kid beating me at my own game! At least you discovered the treasure for me! Give me that!"

Terrified, you look up and see a middle-aged man dressed in a brown jacket with an unlit cigar in his mouth! It's the thug who assaulted the poor antiques dealer!

He tries to snatch the book out of your hands. "Pff. An old book. I would have preferred gold coins or jewelry. But never mind!

Who are you anyway? How did you find me?"

"I . . . I was on duty at the museum."

"Oh, so you've caught me twice! You got me at the museum! I was scared and rushed off, leaving my boot prints in the dirt like an idiot! I thought that old geezer would sleep through it all!"

"Don't talk about my grandfather like that!" you shout, feeling brave again.

"Ha! Ha! Ha! What are you going to do about it? You're just a kid! I'll lock you in a closet like the bad kid you are! And you'll be stuck in there while I escape!"

"But what about the fireworks?"

"Ha! Ha! I'm not a pyrotechnician. That's just an act to get invited to special locations. I pretend to prepare a fireworks display and get behind-the-scenes access to a whole bunch of castles and manors at any time of the day and night, even when they're closed. They even give me the keys! How do you think I got into the castle? People are so naive. I've been doing this awhile."

"But why did you break into the museum? And why did you leave a candy wrapper and a feather?"

"Well, what do we have here—a little detective! Fine, I'll humor you. I thought I needed Knight Lallet's sword—the one in the museum. I noticed that it was missing from the exhibition, so I assumed it was in storage. I knew there'd be an investigation, so I left a feather to point to the butcher and a candy wrapper to point to that stupid fisherman who's in the same hotel as me—and who snores loudly every night, I might add.

I picked up all that false evidence when I had coffee with them in the town."

"Why?"

"Those fake clues would've led the police on a wild goose chase."

"That's horrible. Innocent people would've been falsely accused!"

"Oh, how sentimental. And with my fake name, that stupid English accent, and my disguise at the antiques dealer, I could've almost stayed in town without being discovered! Because of you, though, I have to run! But I'll forgive you since you opened that safe for me. In a way, you're my accomplice."

"That's not true!"

"Okay, it's time for me to go. Let me introduce you to your new home: the broom closet. Come with me and don't make a fuss!"

And this is how you find yourself in the dark, trapped in a room that reeks of cleaning products. Well, it's not completely dark. There's light coming in from under the door. You may be in a closet, but it's better than the dungeon! You look through the keyhole and see the key in the lock on the other side. What if you could knock it out? How would you get the key?

Be quick! Do you have something in your inventory that you could use? Go to your combination table and find a way out of this closet!

161

You slide a sheet of newspaper under the door. But how are you going to push the key out? Your finger is way too big.

Go back to **160** and keep trying! This is a good start!

162

You slide a sheet of newspaper under the door, directly beneath the lock, leaving a little bit of paper on your side. You then unfold the paper clip. With this little tool, you gently push the key out the other side. It falls onto the newspaper. You then slide the newspaper back under the door with the key. You grab the key and unlock the door from the inside. Well done!

Go read the **epilogue** to see what happens next.

163

You try to pick the lock from the inside, but it doesn't work.

Go back to **160** and try again.

164

You strike a match and see all the labels of the chemical bottles around you with flammable warnings. This is dangerous! Blow out that match right now!

Go back to **160** and try again.

EPILOGUE

You open the door and escape from the closet. You blink to get used to the light again. Now be quick! Chase the thief! You sprint back in the direction you came from and catch up with him before he escapes the castle. He's trying to walk out casually, using his pyrotechnician cover. He's almost at the door to the drawbridge. You can't let him get away!

You need an idea! You go quickly to the room with the three levers, including the one you raised earlier to open the gate. You use the one on the right to raise the drawbridge. Through the window hole, you see the thief below. He looks surprised! He tries to run . . . but the wooden drawbridge goes up faster and faster, and he slides backward. He almost has to climb on all fours to keep moving. He looks back at you. You know that he'll try to come after you, and you'll be in trouble! So you lower the lever on the left to close the gate. You've got him locked between the door and the raised drawbridge!

"Help!" he shouts.

Serves him right.

At last, you hear footsteps! The castle keeper and the police are running your way!

"I captured the thief! Don't let him get away," you warn them through the narrow opening. "I'll lower the drawbridge. He's trapped in there."

The police handcuff the thief. Looks like his luck ran out. You open the gate back up and walk out, more than a little proud of yourself.

"Kid! You're okay!" one of the police officers shouts. "The antiques dealer told us what happened to him. What's going on here?"

"The man I trapped is the thief. He robbed the museum, stole that sword from Knight Lallet, and tried to frame innocent people!"

"I can't believe it! But why?"

"To find the castle's treasure—the antique he's got with him. It was hidden in the chess room by Ernest Dumont before the war! He's the one who wrote that story on the fountain. Everybody's read it, but no one understood it until now. You just have to read every fourth word!"

"Wow! You're so brave. You're our very own Sherlock Holmes!"

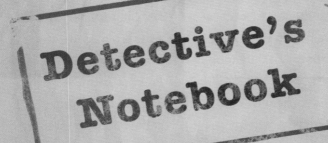

HERITAGE ASSOCIATION LOTTERY

The winner of the Heritage Association lottery is our librarian. Having lived in our fair city since 1996, Elisabeth hit the jackpot! "I always play these same two numbers: 14 Calvados St., where I live, and 50 Manche Ave., where I'm from. They're my lucky numbers," she said.

The Winners

- Elisabeth, number 1450, wins a trip to Mont Saint-Michel for two.
- Daniel, number 0704, wins a barbecue and a set of skewers.
- Patricia, number 2371, wins a ham generously donated by Chilliver's Meats.

EVENTS AT THE CASTLE

This year, the Fourteenth of July fireworks will be launched from the town's castle. Mr. Gadulos, an internationally renowned pyrotechnician, arrived this week to assess and plan the launch systems in the castle and adjoining moat. He has been given full access to the castle so that he can prepare the most beautiful fireworks for the town in complete safety. We hope that our exceptional castle and moat will be complemented by his artistry. The city has housed Mr. Gadulos at the Postal Hotel.

The Chess Room, the castle room famous for its giant chessboard, will soon be the subject of a performance by the children of the town's summer camp.

A2
COMBINATIONS

You can try out your ideas using these tables. You can combine objects to use them together, like opening a chest with a key or using an object in a specific place.

Keypad

0#	0145	1450	1045	1450#	5014	#5014
31	32	33	34	35	32	35

Phone Booth

You need a coin to use the phone. If you don't have any in your inventory, you'll have to keep exploring and come back here later.

31 74 50	31 25 62	31 17 10	31 21 33	31 34 28	31 23 34
44	43	42	41	45	46

Library Computer

5555	8849	233404	2334
39	37	36	38

Dog

Fishing Rod	Bone	Coin	Newspaper
51	53	52	54

Knights

de Cour-seulles	de Rosières	Tilly	Lallet	d'Arché	d'Orville
92	95	96	93	91	94

Castle Gate

Newspaper Paper Airplane	Old Key	Fishing Rod
101	105	103

Hidden Safe

Fishing Rod	Old Key	Paper Clip	Coin
151	153	154	152

Locked in the Closet

Newspaper	Newspaper & Paper Clip	Paper Clip	Match & Newspaper
161	162	163	164

A3
INVENTORY

- [x] Ten-euro bill
- [x] Local newspaper
- [x] Coins
- [x] Fishing rod
- [x] Bone
- [x] Paper clip
- [x] Old key
- [x] Matches

A4
CLUES

The clues are not used in combinations. They're to help you consider important details and solve the investigation.

BEWARE OF RED HERRINGS!

Clue	. . . points to which suspect?
Feather	Butcher
Candy wrapper	fisher men
Footprint	himself
Ash	himself
Library card	
Boots	
List and photograph	

You've managed to succeed this time.

FACE CHALLENGES,

ESCAPE

SOLVE PUZZLES,

BOOK

AND ESCAPE THE BOOK!

. . . Now try your luck
with the rest of the series!